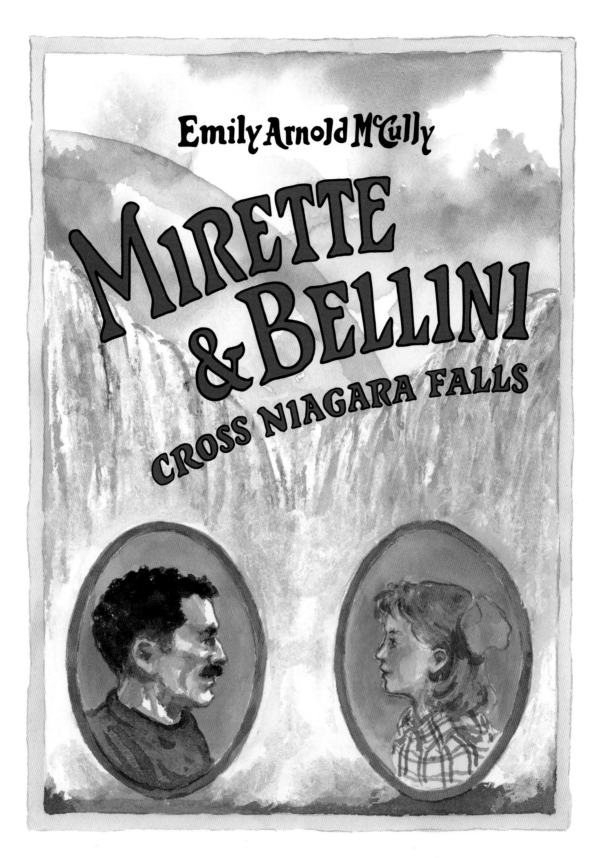

Emily Arnold McCully

MIRETTE & BELLINI CROSS NIAGARA FALLS

G. P. Putnam's Sons ◆ New York

The artwork for this book was created with watercolors and pastels on Arches paper.

Copyright © 2000 by Emily Arnold McCully. All rights reserved. This book, or parts thereof, may not be reproduced in any form without permission in writing from the publisher. G. P. Putnam's Sons, a division of Penguin Putnam Books for Young Readers, 345 Hudson Street, New York, NY 10014. G. P. Putnam's Sons, Reg. U.S. Pat. & Tm. Off. Published simultaneously in Canada. Printed in Hong Kong by South China Printing Co. (1988) Ltd. Lettering by David Gatti. Text set in 14 point Goudy Old Style. Library of Congress Cataloging-in-Publication Data McCully, Emily Arnold. Mirette and Bellini cross Niagara Falls / Emily Arnold McCully. p. cm. Summary: With the help of a young immigrant boy they meet on their crossing to America, two famous tightrope walkers manage to survive the treachery of a rival showman. [1. Aerialists—Fiction. 2. Immigrants—Fiction.] I. Title. PZ7. M478415Mk 2000 [E]—dc21 99-29307 CIP ISBN 0-399-23348-2 10 9 8 7 6 5 4 3 2 1 First Impression

For Steve Gossard, author and curator of
Circus Collections, Illinois State University, Normal,
who kindly provided contemporary newspaper clippings
that made the exploits of real-life high-wire walker Blondin
even more eyepopping.

Every evening, Mirette and Bellini were guests of honor at the Captain's Table on the SS *Magnifique*, bound for New York.

"Let us salute our brave companions," the captain said. "Soon all America will know of their courage and skill."

Mirette and Bellini were the most famous wire walkers in all of Europe. They had just accepted an invitation to cross Niagara Falls.

On calm days, Mirette and Bellini practiced on deck. They could see steerage passengers below, travelling with everything they owned.

One afternoon, Mirette noticed a boy gazing at her with a broad smile. He did a pantomime of wire walking, and applauded himself. Mirette laughed.

The next morning, when Mirette was practicing alone,
the boy suddenly appeared. "Bravo!" he said softly.
He held out a strange little pastry. "For you."
"Thank you," she said.
A steward called out, "You there! Go back where you belong!"
The boy darted off.

At dinner Mirette filled her napkin with fruits and tarts for her new friend. She was sure he would come back, and in the evening, he did. They sat on a stair on the boat deck.

Between bites, Jakob told her he was Polish. His parents had died, and now he was going to live with an uncle in New York.

The next day Mirette introduced Jakob to Bellini. "I, too, was an orphan at your age," Bellini told him.

"I want to become a great man like you," Jakob said. "In America it is possible."

One morning, a few days later, they heard shouts. "Land!" "There she is!" "Miss Liberty!"

The *Magnifique* eased into a berth on the Hudson River. Everyone got off except the steerage passengers, who had to go on to Ellis Island. Mirette was very sorry to be parted from Jakob.

But Bellini surprised her. "We had better stay with Jakob," he said, "until he meets his uncle."

"Move along, stupid!" "Hurry up there!" shouted the officials as they herded the steerage passengers onto a ferry.

"There it is, the Island of Tears," a man said. "If you are sick or no one comes to meet you, they'll send you back."

Mirette and Bellini waited on the balcony of the enormous hall while Jakob was checked. Jakob grinned up at them. Just then, a man pulled him out of the line and they disappeared through a doorway. "That looks like trouble," Bellini said. "Come!"

They found Jakob in a room marked *Special Inquiry*. "He must stay here," an officer said. "No one has come for him. In a few days we'll put him back on a boat." Jakob's eyes welled with tears.

"But he is with me," Bellini said. "He is my assistant."

Bellini signed papers and soon they were on their way.

"We will find your uncle when we get back to New York," said Bellini. "For now, you'll have to come with us."

"I come to New York City and right away I go to Niagara Falls!" Jakob said. "Already I have found opportunity in America!"

They boarded a train that ran along the Hudson River to Albany, then west to Niagara Falls.

Arriving at the station, they saw posters announcing their crossing. But newsboys were shouting, "EXTRA! EXTRA! PATCH SAYS HE WILL SURPASS BELLINI."

"What does this mean?" Mirette asked.

"Apparently this Mr. Patch has challenged us," said Bellini. "If it is a fair contest, we will win."

At the hotel Bellini booked rooms for the week.

"Mr. Patch is already here," the clerk said. "The whole world is coming to see if his crossing is more spectacular than yours."

A man with a notebook said, "I'm from the *New York World*. How will you prove that you are still the world's greatest wire walkers?"

"That will be a surprise," said Bellini.

"Here comes Patch," someone called.

"I am the greatest high-wire walker in America," Patch boasted. "I will perform a feat that no one has ever attempted on the high wire!"

"He has a trick up his sleeve," Bellini whispered to Mirette and Jakob.

While Jakob guarded the door, Bellini and Mirette planned their crossing. "I want to stand on your shoulders," Mirette said. "As I did in Vienna."

"This will be very different from Vienna," Bellini said. "There is the wind, and the noise, and the cable is much longer."

"I can do it," Mirette said.

Outside, Patch was telling reporters that Mirette and Bellini would fall.

On the morning before the crossing Bellini supervised the installation of the wire. A two-thousand-foot length of hemp cable was ferried across the river and stretched from the American to the Canadian bank. It was wound around spools placed in holes drilled into the rock of the cliff and pulled tight by teams of horses. To keep it from swaying, guy wires were attached at twenty-foot intervals and secured to spikes on the shore.

"Get used to the noise and the tumbling of the water," Bellini said. "It will inspire you." And Mirette and Jakob let themselves be filled with the roar of the rapids.

The day of the crossing dawned sunny and mild, with light winds.

Patch had picked a spot for himself downriver. "That gentleman doesn't want anyone to get a good look at his crossing," Bellini said.

"I will go to see if I can find what trick he has in his sleeve," said Jakob, and he ran off along the riverbank.

Patch's camp was heavily guarded. Jakob managed to creep close enough to see that their rival was preparing to cross on a bicycle. But the bicycle was attached to the wire! There was no way Patch could fall! His crossing would look death-defying and yet be perfectly safe.

Jakob raced back to tell Bellini and Mirette. As he ran a movement caught his eye. A man was bending over Mirette and Bellini's central guy wire. When he hurried away, Jakob could see nicks in the wire.

Mirette and Bellini must be warned! Jakob ran as fast as he could . . .

But it was too late! Bellini and Mirette had stepped onto the wire. Jakob shouted but the tumult of the falls drowned his words.

When the crowd saw that Mirette was riding on Bellini's shoulders, people screamed and a few fainted. Bellini walked at a steady pace, the wire vibrating and swaying in the breeze, his balance pole dipping gently up and down.

Downriver, Patch pedaled, raised his arms in the air, reversed a few yards, then inched forward again. He bowed this way and that, to the cheers of his distant supporters.

Jakob started across the bridge.

Mirette and Bellini had reached the middle of the chasm when suddenly their wire jerked violently. Bellini pitched sideways, his balance pole churning the air.

"Slip down on my shoulders!" he shouted. Desperately trying to regain his balance, he broke into a run.

Mirette realized that a guy wire had snapped! Their only hope was to reach the next brace of wires. Bellini ran in a crouch as the rope swung from side to side. The guy wires were just ahead. But one of them, unable to bear the pressure, also snapped! The main rope swerved in the opposite direction!

But Bellini managed to sprint to the last guy wires. They held! Finally Mirette and Bellini ascended the steep incline to the American bank. An excursion boat whistled and the crowd reached out their hands to pull the pair to safety. Men and women cried and the bands blared.

As soon as Mirette and Bellini stepped onto land, reporters shouted questions. "When the guy wires snapped it became extremely difficult," Bellini told them. "But Mirette remained perfectly focused."

"Why do you think they broke?" a reporter called.

Jakob pushed his way through the crowd. "I saw a man cut Bellini's guy wires!" he called. "And Mr. Patch used a trick bicycle!" The crowd gasped.

"Arrest the scoundrel!" people shouted. "Don't let him get away!"

The next day, all the newspapers had pictures of the great crossing—
and of Jakob!

BOY SAW WIRES CUT! BOY NAILS FRAUD!

"Jakob, you're already famous in America!" said Mirette.

Just then there was a knock on the door.

A man stood outside, hat in hand. "Please, is Jakob here? I saw his
picture in this newspaper. I am his uncle, Menachem."

"Here I am!" Jakob cried.

"I was told the wrong boat," Menachem explained. "I waited and
waited and waited!"

"Well, it turned out all right," Mirette said. "Now you and Jakob
have found each other."

They all boarded a train for New York City, grateful for the fortunate turn of events.

When Mirette and Bellini embarked for Europe a few days later, Jakob and Menachem were there to see them off.

"Jakob, you will make a fine American," Bellini said. "As for me, I will be glad to be back in Paris."

"*Au revoir*, dear friend," said Mirette to Jakob. "That means good-bye, until we meet again."